S0-BDP-737
07/22

Nobody Likes Unicorns

To Sage, my favorite critic -KK

To my mom, who loves books -GB

Genius Cat Books

www.geniuscatbooks.com

ABOUT THIS BOOK
The art for this book was created with photoshop and illustrator, using a Wacom Cintiq.
Text was set in Providence Pro and Cortado. It was designed by Germán Blanco.

Library of Congress Control Number: 2021936618

ISBN: 978-1-938447-24-2 (hardcover)

First edition, 2021

Our books may be purchased in bulk for promotional, educational, or business use. For more information, or to schedule an event, please visit geniuscatbooks.com.

Printed and bound in China.

Words: Karen Kilpatrick Pictures: Germán Blanco

Nobody Likes Unicorns

NOBODY likes unicorns.
They are so last year.

12

FIRST:
They only come in one color.

Llamas are way better. We come in lots of different solid and spotted colors like black, gray, tan, brown, red, and white!

But what about their manes?
Oh. Right. I guess they do have colorful rainbow manes...
But let's not focus on that. Moving on!

SECOND: They shed. **EVERYWHERE.**

Llamas are way better. We are super soft and cuddly. In fact, llama wool is light, warm, and water-repellent.

But don't llamas shed, too?
Ugh. How embarrassing.

THIRD:
Unicorns have long, pointy horns.
That's very dangerous!

Llamas are way better. We are huggable and harmless, with no sharp parts anywhere.

But unicorn horns are made to help, not hurt!
I guess I can imagine how their horns could be useful...
And I ♥ s'mores!

FOURTH:

They poop a lot.

It's true! I had a cousin who had a friend that had an uncle who had a teacher who was friends with a unicorn and he told me so!

But it's not ordinary poop.
Really?
Look.
WHAT?!
Unicorns have glittery, rainbow poop?!?

And it smells just like flowers!

FIFTH:

They're really hard to find!

When it comes to llamas, we are **always** here for you.

But I always have a unicorn with me.
Woah! I never knew there were so many adorable unicorn things out there. You can feel together even when you're apart!
Unicorn Power!
Unicorns Rule!

SIXTH:
They claim to be MAGICAL. Magical!
But I've never seen a unicorn do magic.

You just have to make a wish!
They grant wishes?
You're sure?

OK, let's see if this works!

Sweesh!
Wish!
Sneak!
Woosh!

WOW!
I'm a LLAMACORN!!

See, it's true!
Nobody likes unicorns...

BECAUSE EVERYBODY LOVES THEM!

REASONS TO ALSO LOVE LLAMAS

Llamas spit or stick out their tongues when they are annoyed.

One of the ways llamas communicate is by humming.

Llamas are part of the *camelid* family, which means they are closely related to camels!

Llamas can grow up to six feet tall!

While it's not glittery or rainbow-colored, llama poop has almost no odor.

Llamas are great guard animals and are often used to herd sheep!

Dear reader,

We hope you enjoyed this book!

You are now officially a member of the **#GeniusCat** family. What does this mean? Free stuff! Head over to **GeniusCatBooks.com** for a free eBook and a chance to win free print books every month. Plus, you can download activities and educator resources, too.

Please join us on Instagram or Facebook:

@geniuscatbooks

We'll do our best to make it fun!

If you purchased this book from a place where you can leave a review, we would greatly appreciate it if you would give us your honest feedback. It helps the book reach more readers and we love hearing from you!

Our mission is to help foster a lifelong love of reading by publishing books that entertain, inspire, and educate. We're always happy to hear your feedback.

With love,

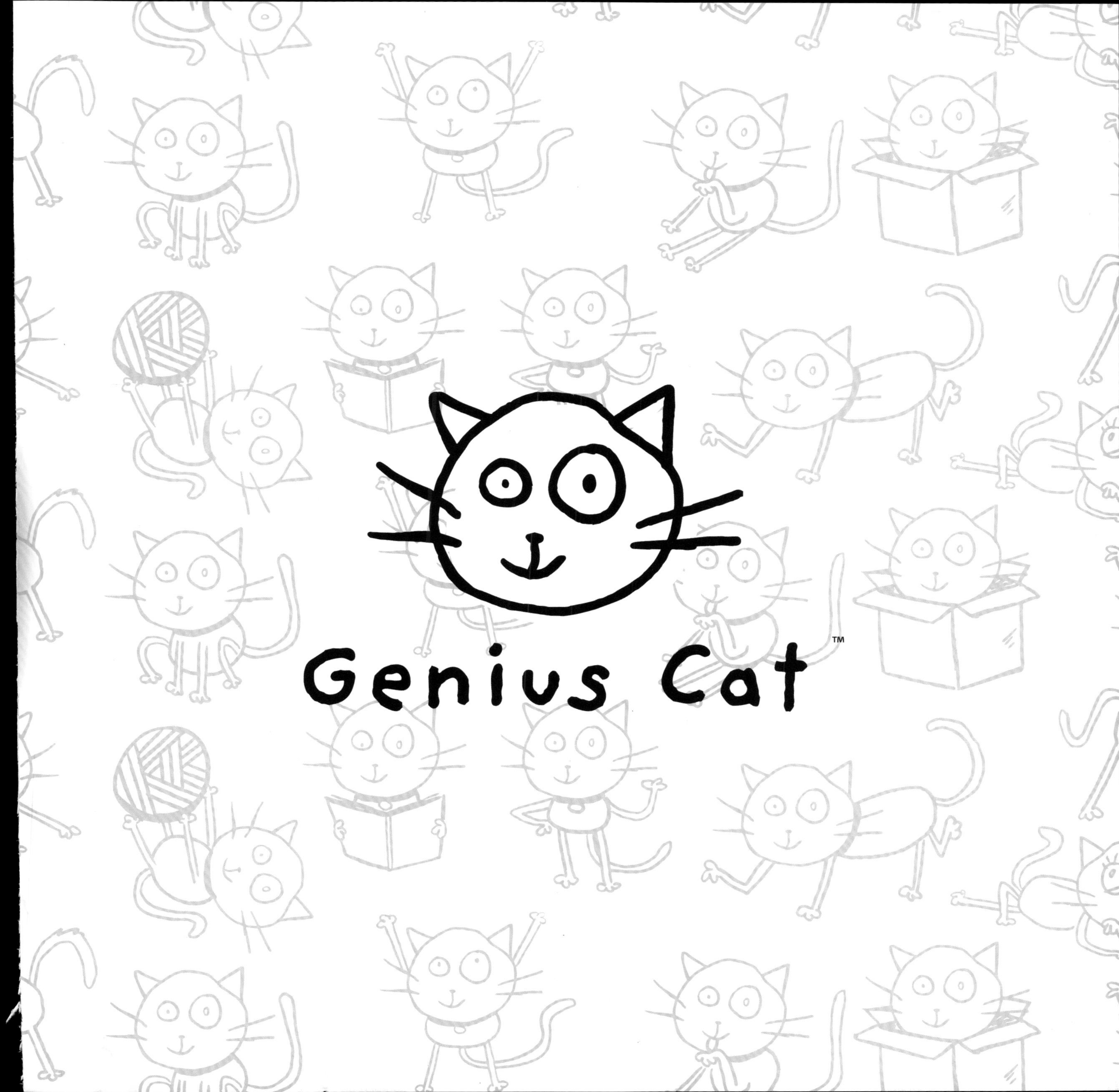
Genius Cat™

Also from Genius Cat

POP!
(September 2021)

Smooch!
(January 2022)

And look out for **Nobody Likes Mermaids**
Coming Spring 2022!